Do

Do YOU see ME on a SAFARI?

Written by

Bonnie G. Busbin

Illustrated by Kimberly Courtney

LANIER
PRESS

LANIER PRESS *an Imprint of BookLogix*

Alpharetta, GA

ISBN: 978-1-6653-0929-5 - Paperback
ISBN: 978-1-6653-0930-1 - Hardcover

These ISBNs are the property of BookLogix for the express purpose of sales and distribution of this title. The content of this book is the property of the copyright holder only. BookLogix does not hold any ownership of the content of this book and is not liable in any way for the materials contained within. The views and opinions expressed in this book are the property of the Author/Copyright holder, and do not necessarily reflect those of BookLogix.

Library of Congress Control Number: 2024914884

♾This paper meets the requirements of ANSI/NISO Z39.48-1992 (Permanence of Paper)

Editor: Bobbie Hinman
Illustrator: Kimberly Courtney

References: www.natgeokids.com; www.nationalgeographic.com; dictionary.com

0 8 1 4 2 4

Let's Go On A Safari!

A *safari* is an adventurous journey to explore or investigate. Often, this adventure takes place in eastern Africa. Most people go on a safari to see amazing jungle animals in their natural *habitats*.

The animals seen on a safari appear to be free, but they fight daily for survival. They search for food and water to stay alive. While searching, they must stay on the lookout for *predators*. Most animals have been created with specific body *adaptations* to help them survive.

Unfortunately, animals cannot protect themselves from the loss of their habitat due to destruction. This is largely why some of the animals in this book are *endangered*, meaning few are left on the earth. Be ready to brainstorm at the end of this book and come up with ways we can help save their homes! We are each a part of the solution.

Now let's go; it's time to start our SAFARI!

All who live in the jungle know I am the KING.
My wild mane proudly wraps 'round my head in a ring.
My great strength is displayed with such courage and pride.
When I ROAR, you are likely to scatter and hide!

Do YOU see ME on a SAFARI?

What am I?

I am a **LION**. Because of my power and strength, I am the king of the jungle. Males have *manes*, but females, called *lionesses*, do not. A thick mane signals that a lion is healthy and tough. The darker the color of the mane, the older the lion. The group we live in is known as a *pride*. A pride may be as small as three or as large as forty lions.

Can you stand on one foot? I can do it with ease.
See, my ankles are where you would think are my knees.
My feathers are pink from the food I ingest . . .
Like the crab, shrimp, and lobster, the treats I like best!

Do YOU see ME on a SAFARI?

What am I?

I am a **FLAMINGO**. I'm an unusual bird. My legs and neck are long and skinny, out of proportion with the rest of my body. Most people mistake my ankles for my knees, but my knees are actually higher up on my legs. My colorful feathers come from the food I eat. When I feed, it is with my head upside down! I am an *omnivore*, eating both meat and plants.

My height scares away predators, a sign of great power.
The group that I live with is known as a **tower**.
My long tongue helps me nibble leaves high on a tree.
I suggest you look up when you're searching for me!

Do YOU see ME on a SAFARI?

What am I?

I am a **GIRAFFE**. It's no surprise I am the tallest living land animal. My lengthy neck helps me be on the lookout for predators. Giraffes use their necks when fighting with one another. My neck, as well as my very long tongue, allows me to reach leaves from tall trees. You may have guessed, but I am a *herbivore*. I do not have to drink much water because I get most of my water from the leaves I eat. However, when thirsty, I must spread my legs far apart and bring my head down to drink. It's quite a sight to see!

Through the day, on the move to seek water and grass,
We confuse all our predators by moving in mass.
We look so much like horses is what I am told.
My black and white stripes are so handsome and bold.

Do YOU see ME on a SAFARI?

What am I?

I am a **ZEBRA**. I look like a horse except for one significant difference—I have black and white stripes. Each zebra has a unique striped pattern. When we are together in a *herd*, our patterns make it difficult for predators to pick out just one zebra in the group. I am a herbivore, meaning I graze on grass and other plants for my meals.

So much has been said about being like you.
With two arms and two legs, it just might be quite true.
I'm a nice, peaceful gent—unless put to the test.
But when challenged, I *SCREAM*, and I beat on my chest.

Do YOU see ME on a SAFARI?

What am I?

I am a **GORILLA**. Many studies have shown the connection between humans and gorillas. We have similar hands, and both of us can use tools. Like many humans, I form strong social bonds and show my emotions. My arms are longer than my legs, and I walk on all fours. This is my "knucklewalk." I don't think man can do that! We live in groups called *troops*.

My trunk travels along wherever I go.
It has so many purposes, not just for show.
It makes noise like a trumpet that's leading a band.
I'm the world's largest animal walking on land.

Do YOU see ME on a SAFARI?

What am I?

I am an **ELEPHANT**. Besides my enormous size, I have many unique features. Most obvious is the large trunk that hangs from my face. It helps me to eat, breathe, drink, and bathe. When I'm swimming, it acts like a snorkel. My trunk is controlled by forty thousand muscles! African elephants' *tusks* grow throughout their lifetime.

The black lines on my face help to block out the sun,
It's amazing to see just how fast I can run.
I have solid black spots on my thick coat of fur.
ROAR? No not me, but I do like to *PURRRR*!

Do YOU see ME on a SAFARI?

What am I?

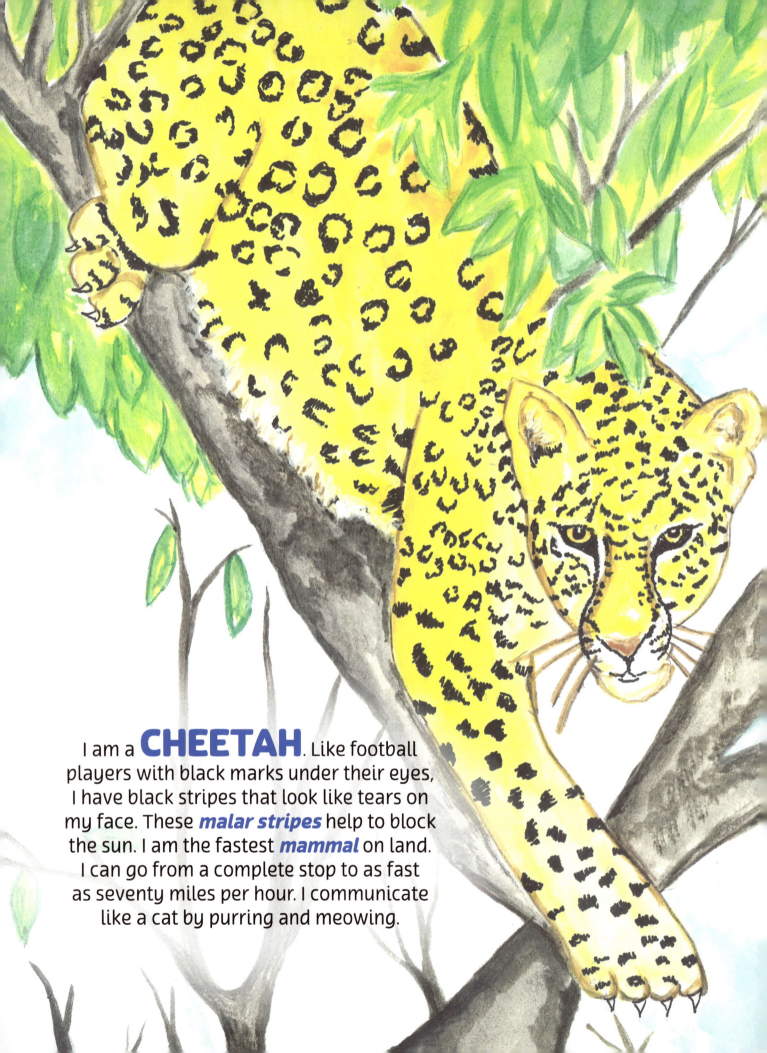

I am a **CHEETAH**. Like football players with black marks under their eyes, I have black stripes that look like tears on my face. These *malar stripes* help to block the sun. I am the fastest *mammal* on land. I can go from a complete stop to as fast as seventy miles per hour. I communicate like a cat by purring and meowing.

While my nose seems to be what attracts those I meet,
Perhaps they should take a look down at my feet.
I have just three toes that bear most of my weight.
Still, the horns on my head are my number one trait.

Do YOU see ME on a SAFARI?

What am I?

I am a **RHINOCEROS**. I am best known for the one or two horns on my snout. As big as I am, it is interesting to note that most of my weight is on just three toes. The middle toe is the strongest. I am a loner and I spend much of my day in a muddy pool, or in the shade trying to stay cool. My name comes from two Greek words: *rhino* (nose) and *ceros* (horn).

I've a long, narrow snout that is shaped like a V.
When it's SNAPPED, there's no way that my *prey* can break free.
Upon seeing my size, you might think I am slow.
But when I'm in the water, watch how fast I can go.

Do YOU see ME on a SAFARI?

What am I?

I am a **CROCODILE**. I am related to the alligator. I am the largest of all living *reptiles*. My snout is narrow, while the alligator's is a broad U-shaped snout. I have the strongest bite of any animal. I spend much of my time in water. I have webbed feet and a flattened tail that propels me up to eighteen miles per hour in the water, beating out an Olympic swimmer!

While most of my hunting is during the night,
My mighty jaws make for a powerful bite.
Celebration begins when I capture my prey.
HA-HA! Yes, a big meal that will start off my day!

Do YOU see ME on a SAFARI?

What am I?

I am a **HYENA**. Most think of laughter when they hear my name. It is true that when I catch my prey, I let out a sound like giggling in celebration of the catch. This sound alerts others I have found food to share. Our group, known as a *cackle*, comes together to help defend our kills from other predators. I have great jaw strength that allows me to tear through bone and meat. Oddly, my back legs are shorter than my front legs, leaving my back slightly sloped.

With a six-foot-wide wingspan, you'd think I could fly!
I am still called a bird, but you must wonder why.
I'm too big and too tall to get up in the air.
And the size of my eggs, you'll admit, is quite rare.

Do YOU see ME on a SAFARI?

What am I?

I am an **OSTRICH**, the largest living bird. I can grow as tall as nine feet, half of which is in my neck. I can run at a very high speed, almost as fast as a racehorse. My wings help keep me balanced while I am running, and also keep me cool. My height helps me see the danger ahead. I have a powerful kick that can kill a predator. An ostrich egg can be six inches round and weigh three pounds.

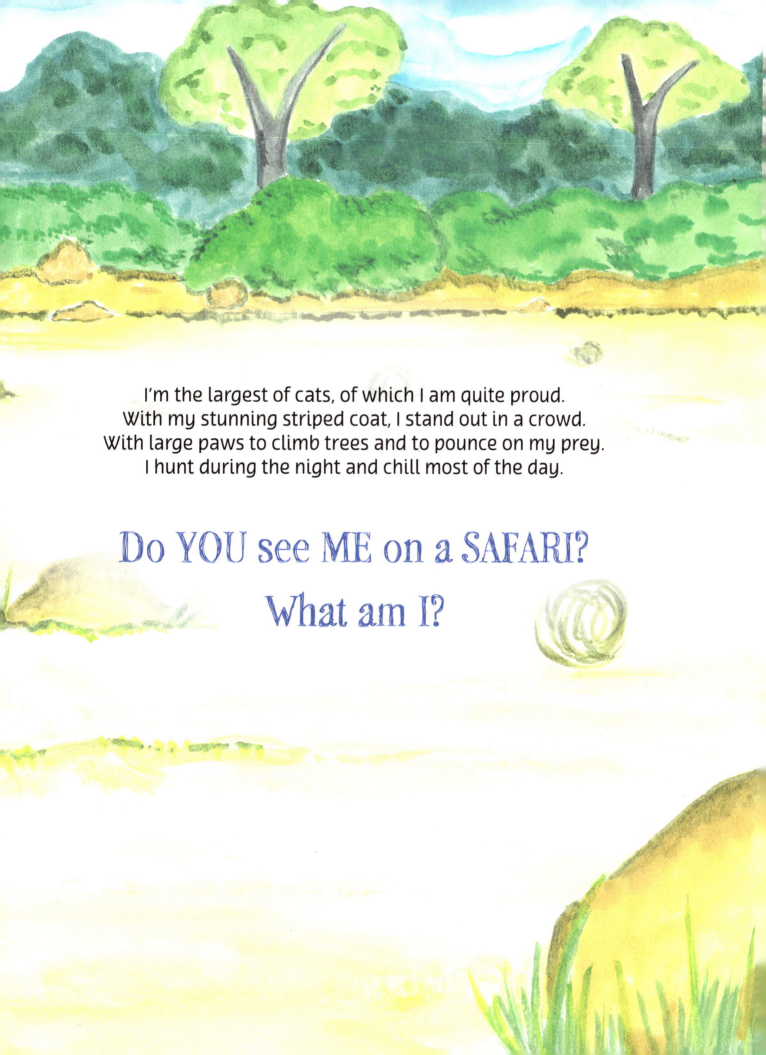

I'm the largest of cats, of which I am quite proud.
With my stunning striped coat, I stand out in a crowd.
With large paws to climb trees and to pounce on my prey.
I hunt during the night and chill most of the day.

Do YOU see ME on a SAFARI?

What am I?

I am a **TIGER**, the largest cat in the world. My beautiful striped coat aids in *camouflaging* me during the hunt. I am a *carnivore* and can survive on one large meal a week. Tigers are strong swimmers and we enjoy being in the water to cool off. My tail can be as long as three feet and I use it to help me stay balanced.

What Do You Think?

Parents and teachers may use these questions to further discuss the animals in this book. There are no right or wrong answers!

Q: After learning about all the animals we might see on a safari, is there one you want to discover more about? Explain why. Is there one animal that is your least favorite? Explain why.

A: Allow the children to express their favorite and least favorite animal from the book or elsewhere.

Q: What do animals need to survive? What adaptations were discussed that helped these animals stay alive? Think of the weather, predators, etc.

A: All animals need food and water to live. Animals have been created with various adaptations to help them stay alive. Camouflage is a modification to an animal's body to help them survive. What else in the book was mentioned to help animals find food and stay alive? (Hint: The elephant's trunk helps it to bathe, stay cool, and eat; how about the others?)

Q: Do you think most animals would prefer to be free? How about our pets? Which do you think has the best life—the free animals or the pets?

A: Most pets (cats and dogs) survive best by living with a family that loves and cares for them. The animals in this book are free in their space but have trials to overcome. Discuss the pros and cons of being free in the wild.

Q: The number one reason animals become endangered or can no longer survive on our planet is the loss of their habitat. What can we do to help protect animal habitats? Think about all the animals found in the wild.

A: Let children know they can participate in the change. By teaching them ways to help our environment (recycling, reducing energy usage), they will understand they can be a part of the solution. Visit an animal shelter or wildlife center that cares for endangered species and discover more ways to help. Brainstorm ways to help!

New Vocabulary Words

Adaptation – adjustments made to help one survive their environment

Cackle – a group of hyenas living together

Camouflage – a coloring, or pattern, that disguises an animal, making it difficult for predators to see them

Carnivore – an animal that eats meat and fish as their primary source of food

Endangered – having a high risk of no longer existing

Habitat – the place where an animal lives

Herbivore – an animal that feeds on grass and other plants

Herd – several animals living and traveling together

Lioness – a female lion

Malar stripes – the dark stripes running from the cheetah's eyes down its face that help to keep the sun away from its eyes

Mammal – animals with backbones, most of their bodies are covered with hair, and the mother feeds her young with milk from her body

Mane – the long hair growing around the neck of a lion

Omnivore – an animal whose diet includes both plants and animals

Predator – an animal that hunts other animals primarily for food

Prey – an animal hunted and captured for food

Pride – a group of lions

Reptile – a cold-blooded vertebrate that crawls or creeps

Safari – a journey or expedition

Tower – a group of giraffes

Troop – a group of gorillas

Tusk – a long pointed or protruding tooth

Author

Bonnie Busbin has a bachelor of science degree in education from Auburn University. As a classroom teacher for twenty-seven years, Bonnie often created riddles, like the ones in this book, for her students. This is the third in the *Do YOU see ME?* Series. The previous books, *Do YOU see ME in the SEA?* and *Do YOU see ME at NIGHT?* follow the same interactive format, creating a bond between the reader and listener. Children will be amazed to learn such interesting facts about God's creatures. Bonnie and her husband reside in Alpharetta, Georgia, and they have two grown children, who are also in education, and five grandchildren.

gchildrenbooks.com

Illustrator

Kim Courtney graduated from the University of Georgia with a bachelor of science degree in art education. She has been teaching art for the past twenty-nine years. When she is not teaching, she is creating art and raising her daughter in Woodstock, Georgia.

Printed in the USA
CPSIA information can be obtained
at www.ICGtesting.com
CBHW041526081024
15567CB00016B/75